Kitten Club

Truffle's Secret Hideaway

STRIPES PUBLISHING
An imprint of Magi Publications
1 The Coda Centre, 189 Munster Road,
London SW6 6AW

A paperback original
First published in Great Britain in 2011

Text copyright © Sue Mongredien, 2011
Illustrations copyright © Artful Doodlers, 2011
Photographs copyright © iStockphoto.com, 2011

ISBN: 978-1-84715-163-6

A CIP catalogue record for this book is available
from the British Library.

Printed and bound in the UK.

10 9 8 7 6 5 4 3 2 1

Sue Mongredien

Kitten Club

Truffle's Secret Hideaway

stripes

Meet the Kitten Club girls!

Amy
& Ginger

Mia
& Smoke

Molly
& Truffle

Ella
& Honey

Ruby
& Ziggy

Lily
& Buster

Chapter 1

"Harvey! Oh, Harvey, no, stop it!" Molly Evans yanked at the dog's collar, trying to drag him away from her kitten's feeding bowl. Harvey looked up at her, his big brown eyes guilty at having been caught, and his tail sagged in dismay. "You know that's not yours," Molly scolded. "Poor Truffle! That's her food, it's not for you!"

Harvey gave a whine as if to say sorry, and slunk across to the back door, whimpering to be let outside. Molly sighed as she opened the door and watched him lollop into the garden. Harvey was the greediest dog in the world! He had this awful habit of staring intently at Molly or her brothers whenever they ate a meal, hoping for a titbit, and lately he had taken to scoffing down Truffle's kitten food too.

Truffle hadn't eaten much breakfast that morning and Harvey had been only too pleased to gobble down the rest.

Where *was* Truffle, anyway? It was Saturday, and Molly had been looking forward to spending time with her super-cute kitten. Truffle had pretty stripey tabby fur, a white bib and little white feet, like socks. When Molly had first got her, Truffle had been so tiny she could fit in Molly's hand, but she was four months old now, and starting to look less kitteny and more like a cat.

It was nearly time for today's Kitten Club meeting, but Molly wanted to make sure Truffle was OK before her friend Lily arrived to pick her up. Molly had last seen her kitten before lunch, when Truffle had been curled

up asleep in one of the flowerbeds, enjoying a welcome burst of November sunshine. But where was she now?

Just then Molly heard a shout from outside, followed by some excited woofing. "And it's a goooooalllll! United score again! Daniel Evans is on top form today!"

Molly glanced out of the window. Two of her brothers, Luke and Daniel, were playing football in the garden, and Harvey had joined them. He seemed to have completely forgotten his ticking-off and was gambolling about like a loon, his tail wagging excitedly.

Surprise, surprise, Truffle was no longer asleep in the flowerbed. She was rather scared of Molly's brothers, and whenever they were in the garden, Truffle would run away to find

a quieter spot. Hopefully she'd found
somewhere peaceful to doze inside, or…

Then Molly stared. Oh no! Truffle
wasn't inside at all. She was up a tree, scared
to death, clinging to the branch with her
tiny claws. Her fur was fluffed up and her
eyes were round and anxious. Every time
the boys shouted or Harvey woofed, she
hunched closer to the branch in fright.

Molly was just about to run and rescue her when the telephone started ringing, and then the doorbell chimed too. "I'll get the phone," her mum called from the next room. "Can somebody answer the door?"

Molly hesitated, wanting to rush out and help Truffle, but she could hear music blasting from her eldest brother's bedroom and guessed that he wouldn't have heard the doorbell. She knew Dad was doing something in the garage, and Luke and Daniel were still outside. That only left her to answer the door. "Back in a minute, Truffle," she murmured, hurrying into the hall.

It was Lily at the door, and Molly could see Lily's mum in the car outside, with baby Jessica strapped into her car seat. "Hi," Lily said, smiling. "Are you ready to go?"

"Nearly," Molly said. "I've just got to
help Truffle down from a tree in the
garden. I'll be two minutes, OK?"

"Oh no, poor Truffle! OK, I'll tell Mum,
then I'll come and help you," Lily said.

Molly slipped on her trainers and dashed
back into the garden, ducking to avoid being
hit by the football. "Watch it!" she shouted,
hurrying towards the tree where Truffle had
been earlier. But Truffle had gone.

"Oh!" Molly said in surprise. "Luke, Dan, did you see where Truffle went?"

Twelve-year-old Luke couldn't quite look Molly in the eye. "Well, the thing was…" he began shiftily.

"It was an accident!" Daniel blurted out. He was ten, two years older than Molly and had the same dark hair and brown eyes as her.

"What was an accident? What happened?" Molly asked, putting her hands on her hips.

"Well, we were just playing football when the ball kind of…" Luke scuffed his foot along the grass. "It kind of slammed into the tree," he finished after a moment.

"What, and Truffle fell out of it?" Molly asked in horror, imagining her poor kitten plunging from the branch.

"No, she just freaked out and jumped into next door's garden," Daniel said. "It was an accident!" he repeated, seeing Molly's cross face.

"Have you got her?" Lily asked, appearing just then.

Molly shook her head. "These two scared her away," she said crossly, her fingers curling into fists. She wished she had time to try and tempt Truffle home again, but she knew Lily's mum was waiting. "Come on, let's go," she muttered, stomping back through the house. "Mum, I'm going to Kitten Club! See you later!"

she called as she grabbed her coat on her way out of the door.

She couldn't help shuddering as she imagined the football crashing into the tree and frightening poor Truffle. She hoped Truffle hadn't hurt herself jumping from such a height.

"Hi, Molly," Lily's mum said as the girls clambered in. "Are we all set for Kitten Club, then, you two?"

"Yeah!" Lily cheered, clipping in her seat belt. "Let's go!"

Chapter 2

It was Amy's turn to host the Kitten Club meeting. There were six girls in the club, and they'd met when they were choosing their kittens at Chestnut Farm back in the summer. Lily had had the brilliant idea of forming a club where they could get together every week to talk about their new pets. Everyone had loved Lily's suggestion

and they'd met up every Saturday since.

The other girls were already there when Molly and Lily arrived. Amy's mum showed them through to the kitchen where Amy, Ella, Mia and Ruby were sitting at the table.

"Hi, guys," Molly said, as she and Lily joined them. "Oh, hello, Ginger – I didn't see you there!" she added, as she pulled out the chair to find Amy's marmalade-coloured kitten having a snooze.

"I nearly sat on you." She stroked him, and he opened his eyes a crack and purred.

"Hi, Moggy, hi, Scatty," Amy said, using the special Kitten Club code names to address Molly and Lily. "Ginger's been warming your seat for you. Scoop him on to your lap, he won't mind."

Molly carefully lifted the warm ginger bundle and sat down, settling him on her knee. Ginger gave another rumbling purr and cuddled up to her. The way he tucked himself into the crook of her arm reminded Molly of Truffle. Where had she gone? She hoped her kitten had found some peace and quiet.

"Hi, guys," Mia said, smiling. She had their Kitten Club scrapbook in front of her and opened it on to a new page. "Shall we do our roll-call now that everyone's here?"

"Let's," agreed Ruby, who was Molly's best friend from school, and was dressed as

usual in pink from head to toe.

"OK, then. Tomboy?" said Mia.

"Meow," said blonde-haired Ella, then added a throaty purring sound which made everyone laugh.

"Green-Eyes?"

"Meow," said Amy, who did have lovely green eyes, just like a cat.

"Glamour-Puss?"

"Meow," said Ruby.

"Moggy?"

"Meow," Molly said with a grin.

"Witch-Cat – meow, I'm here," Mia said, ticking off her own name. "And finally … Scatty."

"Meow d'ya do?" Lily said, which made everyone laugh again. Lily loved having an audience!

The girls swapped their kitten news over lemonade and home-made jam tarts. Ella was pleased to report that her kitten, Honey, was getting on much better with Misty, her family's older cat. Previously, Misty had often lashed out in annoyance at excitable Honey. But a week ago, Misty had actually leaped to Honey's rescue when the kitten was being bullied by a neighbour's cat, and Ella had been hopeful of a truce. "Since then, they seem to be getting on OK," Ella said.

"Misty gave Honey a smack the other day for jumping on her tail, but that's the only trouble we've had so far. Thank goodness!"

"Well, Buster's had a smack or two lately as well," Lily said, grimacing. "Poor boy! I think he always thought Jessica, my little sister, was a bit boring because she never did anything except lie on her baby mat, or cry. But now she's learned how to crawl…"

"Uh-oh," said Mia, who had a little sister too. "I bet Buster's not happy about that."

"He is *so* not happy!" Lily said, rolling her eyes. "And now she thinks it's the best game ever to follow Buster around the house, trying to grab his tail.

Or, even worse, crawling up to him when he's asleep and trying to kiss and cuddle him!"

The others laughed at Lily's horrified expression. "Poor Buster," Ruby said. "My brother Max used to think Ziggy was a toy at first too. Maybe you could get a toy cat for Jessica? That's what Mum did. She'd say, 'No, Max, this is your cat,' and hand him a stuffed one whenever he started hassling Ziggy."

"That's a good idea," Lily said. "Anything to give Buster a break. Jessica's quite a fast crawler already. Buster climbed the curtains yesterday, trying to escape her. Mum wasn't too pleased about that…"

"Smokey also likes a bit of curtain climbing." Mia grinned. "And my mum gets cross too! Especially when he did a flying leap from the curtain pole on to her shoulder.

She screamed so loud I thought the house must be on fire!"

"Ginger had a climbing adventure recently too – he got stuck up in the cherry tree," Amy put in. She glanced out at the garden where the wind was buffeting the tree's bare branches, making them rattle. "Silly boy. He climbed really high, then lost his nerve. Dad had to get a ladder and rescue him."

"Oh, Ginger," Ruby said, reaching over to tickle his neck. "Was it a bit scary up in that horrid old tree, then?"

Ginger purred as Ruby stroked him. Molly said nothing. She was thinking about Truffle being up the tree earlier, and how

the boys had frightened her out of it.
At least Ginger hadn't had to worry about
that. She sighed, hoping Truffle was OK.
It couldn't be easy being a little kitten and
having to share a house with Molly and her
brothers, not to mention their dog, two
guinea pigs and a hamster as well.

"Everything all right, Moggy?" Amy
asked, hearing Molly's sigh.

Molly tried to smile, but it didn't quite
work. "Yeah," she said. "Well, actually, no,"
she corrected herself. "Not really. I'm worried
about Truffle. I don't think she's very happy."

"Why? What's wrong?" Mia asked,
sounding surprised.

"Well, you know what a sleepyhead she
is," Molly said. "She loves finding warm, cosy
spots for catnaps. But there's always so much

going on in our house that she's often woken up and frightened off. My brothers are either playing loud music or noisy football games, and Harvey keeps helping himself to her food. It's like she's getting pushed out of her own home." Molly bit her lip. "Ever since Truffle's been able to go outside, I've seen less and less of her. I don't know where she goes, but sometimes she's away for hours."

"That could just mean she's adventurous," Ella suggested. "Maybe she likes exploring. Cats are really independent like that."

"Yes, Smokey goes off for hours at a time as well," Mia said. "I bet Truffle's just checking out the big wide world, that's all."

Molly shook her head. Smokey might be a brave explorer, but Truffle was more of a cuddle-cat, who liked her creature comforts.

"I don't think so," Molly replied. "If it was down to her, she'd spend the whole day snoozing on my bed. Her going off for hours isn't because she's adventurous, it's because she's desperate to get out of our madhouse." She put her head in her hands, the words spilling out. "I'm worried she doesn't like living with such a crazy, loud family. I bet she wishes one of you guys had chosen her instead of me, so she could live in one of your nice quiet houses instead!"

Chapter 3

There was a stunned silence at Molly's outburst. Then Ruby put her arm around Molly and hugged her. "No way!" she said staunchly. "Of course she doesn't think that. You've always looked after her really well, Molly. She loves having you as her kitten-mummy!"

Molly gave a sniff. She wasn't the sort of

person who'd burst into tears at the drop of a hat, but all the same, she had a horrible prickly feeling at the back of her throat as if she might very well start crying. "Truffle's not been eating much lately, either," Molly said. "And last night, I was looking on a kitten website that Dad found for me and saw that a kitten being off their food is a sign that they're not well – or really, really unhappy!"

"Maybe it's because her bowl smells of Harvey," Lily suggested. "You said that he'd been tucking into her food – maybe his doggy smell is putting her off."

"Could you shut him outside while you're feeding Truffle, maybe?" Mia suggested. "Then she can eat in peace without him around."

"Yes, and you could shut Harvey in when Truffle wants to go outside," Ella added. "Since we began trying to keep Honey and Misty apart more often, they're definitely happier."

"Those are good ideas," Molly said, nodding. "I'll try them. I just want Truffle to enjoy living with me as much as I enjoy living with her." She gave a watery smile. "Thanks, guys. What would I do without you?"

"Oh, you'd probably be completely miserable," Lily assured her with a grin, giving Molly's hand a squeeze.

Molly laughed, feeling a bit better. Lily was joking of course, but Molly did feel lucky to have her Kitten Club friends.

Just then, Amy put some paper and some felt-tip pens on the table. "I was thinking

about what we could do today," she said. "Why don't we make a kitten magazine? We can put in news stories and photos, a puzzle page—"

"Kitten horoscopes!" Ruby interrupted, giggling.

"Drawings and cartoons," Mia said excitedly.

"Facts about kittens and tips for kitten care," Ella suggested.

"Kitten jokes!" Lily put in.

"And a problem page for anxious owners," Molly said with a little laugh. "That's what I need!"

"What a cool idea, Amy," Ruby said. "Let's get started!"

Amy beamed. "Mum says she'll photocopy it at work when we've finished," she added. "That way we can all have a copy. We could stick a copy in our scrapbook too."

"What shall we call it?" Mia wondered. "*The Kitten Club Times?*"

"How about *The Cat's Meow?*" Lily giggled. "Or just *MEOW!* like one of those celebrity magazines my mum reads?"

Everybody liked this idea. "Who's going to do our front page?" Ella asked. "Mia, you're really good at art – do you want to design it?"

Mia nodded, pleased. "Definitely!" she said. "What's everyone else going to do?"

"I'll write some news stories," Ruby

offered. She loved English lessons at school, and had the neatest handwriting too.

"I could do a kitten care article," Amy suggested. "Including something about not feeding them too much!"

Molly smiled at her. When Amy had first got Ginger, she'd doted on him so much she'd ended up overfeeding him, and he'd ballooned out. "I'll do a kitten crossword," Molly said, grabbing a pen. "And maybe a wordsearch too, filled with lots of kitten words – and all our kittens' names."

Everyone got stuck in. Ella began drawing a cartoon strip, and Lily put together a page of jokes, which she insisted on trying out on the others. "What happened to the cat who ate a ball of wool?" she asked with a grin.

"I don't know," chorused Mia and Molly.

"She had mittens!" Lily chuckled, making everyone groan.

Molly chewed the end of her pen as she thought of her first crossword clue. Then she smiled. *Where we got our kittens from*, she wrote, and counted the letters on her fingers. C-H-E-S-T-N-U-T F-A-R-M, she spelled. Eight letters, then four. She was off!

It started raining after a while — a horrible grey drizzle that made Molly feel

glad to be warm and dry in Amy's cosy kitchen, making the *MEOW!* magazine with the Kitten Club girls. She felt glad too for pouring out her worries to her friends. They'd had some good ideas that could help the problem, and Molly was already planning to try them out once she was back home. With a bit of luck, Truffle would soon feel like the most chilled-out and best-loved kitten in the whole country.

Chapter 4

The girls were all enjoying working on their magazine so much that the afternoon flew by, and all of a sudden, some of the parents had arrived to take them home. "Let's carry on with our magazine stuff separately this week and bring it to the next meeting," Lily suggested.

Molly's mum was there to take her,

Lily and Ruby back to their homes, and overheard Lily. "Do you want to have the next meeting at ours?" she asked, tousling Molly's hair. "I'll make sure those noisy boys of mine are out of your way, OK?"

"Sounds good," Ella said with a smile. She had a twin brother who was almost as annoying as Molly's brothers.

Molly, Lily and Ruby said goodbye to the others, and went out to the car. "Mum, has Truffle been around this afternoon?" Molly asked, crossing her fingers hopefully.

"Truffle? Yes, she was in your bedroom earlier," her mum replied. "I went in to hoover, and she was asleep on your beanbag. I didn't have the heart to disturb her." She grinned. "Well, that's my excuse for not doing the hoovering, anyway."

"Phew!" Molly said, feeling relieved.

They dropped off Ruby, then drove home. Lily lived on the same street as Molly and the two girls were in and out of each other's houses all the time. "Can I pop in to see Truffle?" Lily asked.

"Of course," Molly's mum said. "Stay for tea if you want – I'll let your mum know."

Molly and Lily went upstairs to Molly's room, where Truffle was still fast asleep on Molly's beanbag. "Hello, sweetie," Molly said softly. Truffle gave a sleepy mew, as if saying hello back, then purred as Molly gently stroked her tabby fur.

"Now that doesn't look like a miserable kitty to me," Lily said, crouching down next to Molly. "Look at her, she's as happy as me in a sweet shop."

Molly smiled. Truffle did look happy, it was true. Then she noticed something. "Oh, Truffle! Your collar's come off *again*," she exclaimed. "Where have you lost it this time?" She turned to Lily. "It must be a bit big because it's come off a few times." She tickled Truffle under the chin. "We need to get you a smaller one, don't we?"

Lily stroked her as well, and soon Truffle's body was rumbling with purrs. "She looks really healthy too," Lily said. "I know you said she was off her food, but she doesn't look ill – or skinny. She seems fine."

The girls left Truffle to go back to sleep and went on a hunt for the missing collar. It had stopped raining by now so they went into the garden where they finally found the soggy, muddy blue collar on the lawn. "Yuck," Molly said, picking it up gingerly. "It must have been out here all afternoon. It's soaking!"

Once inside, Molly rinsed the mud off the collar and put it on the kitchen radiator to dry. Her mum and dad were preparing the vegetables for tea and listening to the radio. "Mum, can we get Truffle a new collar?" Molly asked. "This one's too big, and it keeps falling off her."

"Sure," Molly's mum said, dumping potato peelings into the compost bin. "I'll pick one up next time I'm in town."

Molly and Lily went back up to Molly's room, but just then Alfie, who had the bedroom next door, began blasting music through the wall. Truffle woke up in alarm, her eyes wide and her ears flattened back as if she were about to bolt off. "Come on, let's get you away from that racket," Molly said, quickly scooping her up before she shot away elsewhere. "We'll play with you downstairs instead."

Molly and Lily spent a while pulling a
string up and down the hall for the excited
kitten to scamper after and pounce on.
Harvey was safely shut away, and the other
boys were glued to the PlayStation, so for
once Truffle could have a good play
without being disturbed.

"See?" said Lily after tea when it was time for her to go home. "She *is* happy, Molly. She loves living here with you." She leaned over to stroke Truffle, who was snuggled up in Molly's arms. "See you, gorgeous!"

"Bye, Lily," Molly said, feeling much more cheerful. But as the front door shut behind Lily, the telephone rang and Harvey started barking. Truffle immediately leaped out of Molly's arms and fled upstairs. Molly rolled her eyes. Typical! She should have known the peace and quiet couldn't last long in the Evans's home!

On Tuesday, Ruby came round for tea after school. It was chilly but still sunny so the girls went into the garden to play with Truffle.

Molly found a small rubber ball and
bounced it on the path, and Truffle, eyes
wide with delight, chased it like a wild thing,
her little paws slipping on its round surface.
Molly had put her collar back on, and its
bell jingled madly as she ran.

Molly and Ruby laughed at her – but
then out bounded Harvey, his tail wagging
excitedly as he rushed over.

"Oh no," Molly groaned. She'd forgotten to shut the back door so that he couldn't come out. She hurried to grab his collar before he could startle Truffle, but she was too late; Harvey was already running towards the ball, eager to join in the fun. In a flash, Truffle was off, scrambling to get away from the big dog, almost falling off the fence in her desperation to escape.

Harvey barked excitedly and Truffle jumped off the fence, disappearing into the neighbours' garden. Harvey's tail drooped as if he was disappointed she'd gone.

"Oh, Harvey," Molly said, sighing as she patted him. "I know you're just being friendly, but…" His plumey tail wagged and he licked her face. "Come on, inside you go. Just till we can coax Truffle back."

She led Harvey into the house and closed the door, then she and Ruby called Truffle, hoping the kitten's sweet little face would reappear over the fence. It didn't. "Truffle, come on," Molly pleaded. "Harvey's gone, it's just us."

"Truffle, come and play!" Ruby called.

But it was no use. Truffle didn't come, even though the girls spent ages calling her.

After a while, purple-black clouds scudded across the sky and a light rain began to fall.

She and Ruby trooped indoors. "Why don't we write something new for the magazine?" Ruby suggested. "We could do some silly kitten horoscopes, with pictures to go with each one. What do you think?"

"Good idea," Molly replied, getting out some paper and pens. Hopefully writing horoscopes would distract her from worrying about Truffle.

"OK, let's start with Aries," Ruby said. "Aries is the sign of the ram, isn't it? So maybe we could put something like 'You might find yourself saying "Baaaa" instead of "Meow" this week.'" She giggled. "Or even, '*ewe*' might find yourself saying it – ewe, do you get it?"

She wrote it down, still giggling, but Molly felt as if her sense of humour had deserted her. She couldn't help becoming increasingly uneasy as the sky grew darker outside. Where had Truffle gone?

Truffle didn't reappear all afternoon. She didn't even come in for her tea. The girls tried calling from the back door again after they'd eaten, shining torches down the dark garden, but there was no sign of her.

Finally, when it was almost time for

Ruby to go home, Truffle crept warily
through the cat flap, looking all around with
big eyes as if checking the coast was clear.

"There you are!" Molly cried in relief,
cuddling her. "Thank goodness you're
back!" She pressed her head against
Truffle's cold damp fur, and could feel her
kitten's heart racing. Poor Truffle! Was it
really so bad here in the house that she'd
rather be outside?

Ruby stroked the kitten's head. "Phew! You had us worried, Truffle," she said. "You and your adventures – you're as bad as Ziggy."

Molly knew Ruby was trying to make her feel better, but she also knew that Ziggy was a cheeky, fearless kitten with a permanent glint of mischief in his eye, whereas Truffle was a big softie. But lately, Truffle had turned from being a softie into a real scaredy-cat. Somehow Molly had to make her feel more at home and less scared. But how?

Chapter 5

Molly did her best to give Truffle plenty of peace and quiet over the next few days. When her brothers practised penalty shoot-outs in the hall the next evening, as it was raining outside, she took Truffle upstairs to her bedroom so that she wouldn't be scared by the clanging of the ball against the radiator and the boys' whoops and yells

– not to mention Dad's shouts when he ordered them to stop playing. She brushed Truffle until her fur shone like silk and in return, Truffle purred like a little engine. Molly also made sure that Harvey wasn't around whenever she fed Truffle, so that Truffle could eat without Harvey shoving his greedy face in the bowl alongside hers.

"I think things have been much better lately," Molly told Ruby and Amy on Friday at school. "I feel like I'm Truffle's guardian angel, leaping in to protect her whenever something's about to scare her. But it's working! I'm sure she's happier now."

"Oh, that's good," Amy said. "And it's Kitten Club tomorrow at yours, isn't it? We can all make a big fuss of her then."

"I know, I can't wait," Molly said. "Dad's taking my brothers and Harvey out all afternoon so it'll be just us girls and Truffle. And as soon as I get back tonight I'm going to find Truffle and play with her non-stop until bedtime."

Unfortunately, when Molly got home later on, her mum had other ideas. "Molly, it's your turn to clean out the guinea pigs and hamster," Mrs Evans reminded her.

Molly groaned but knew she had to do it. Her parents were really strict about them looking after their pets properly. She cuddled Truffle and took her up to her bedroom, settling her down on the beanbag.

"I've just got to clean out some stinky cages and then I'll be back to play with you," she promised. "You wait here for me. I'll be as quick as I can."

Molly took a bin bag and some newspapers into the utility room and began cleaning out the cages. She put down fresh sawdust for Biscuits the hamster, and clean straw for Sindy and Snowy the guinea pigs. She rinsed and refilled their water bottles and fed them, and then she was done. At last!

She heaved the rubbish into the dustbin and washed her hands. But when she went back to her bedroom, Truffle had vanished. Alfie was blaring his music through the wall again so Molly guessed that the noise had scared Truffle downstairs. As usual!

"Alfie!" she heard Mum yelling. "Alfie! Turn that music down!"

Alfie didn't seem to hear, though, or if he did, Molly guessed he was ignoring Mum. She ran downstairs to find Truffle, and saw her brother Daniel whizzing about on rollerblades in the hall. "Have you seen Truffle anywhere?" she asked him.

He did a spin at one end, then came to a stop. "Yeah, I nearly ran over her a few minutes ago," he said. "She just appeared from out of nowhere and I had to shout at her to move."

"You had to shout at her?" Molly echoed in dismay.

Daniel shrugged. "Well, it was that or flatten her tail, so yeah. She ran into the living room, I think."

Molly trudged into the living room to find Luke and his friends playing a noisy football game on the PlayStation.

"Have you seen Truffle?" she asked Luke.

His eyes were on the TV screen. "Shoot – shoot!" he yelled, then groaned as, on-screen, the ball whacked against the crossbar.

"Unlucky, mate. What? Truffle?" he said finally, turning round to Molly. "Um … yeah. She wandered in just as Joel scored a few minutes ago."

"And then what happened?" Molly asked, but Luke was looking at the screen.

"PENALTY!" he roared. "Definitely a penalty! Er… Well, we all cheered, and I think that scared her off. She ran away towards the kitchen."

Molly gritted her teeth. "OK," she said, striding into the kitchen. Her mum was in there preparing tea and listening to the radio. She looked up when Molly came in.

"All done? Thanks, love," she said.

"Have you seen Truffle, Mum?" Molly asked her.

"Yes, she just went out of the cat flap two minutes ago," her mum replied. "Would you mind setting the table, please? There'll be eight of us tonight, with Joel and Nathan staying."

But Molly wasn't listening. She'd just noticed that the back door was open, and that Harvey was in the garden, woofing. "Oh no," she sighed. "Mum, did you let Harvey out with Truffle?"

Her mum frowned at something on the radio. "Hold on, I just want to catch this bit of the news," she murmured, turning up the volume.

Molly's shoulders slumped. "Never mind," she said, hurrying into the garden. Harvey bounded up to her ... but Truffle was nowhere in sight. Molly sat on the back

step, patting Harvey and feeling really bad as she imagined Truffle going from one place to another through the house, trying to find a peaceful spot, but being continually scared away. And now she'd gone!

Molly shut Harvey back in the house and called for her kitten. "Truffle! Where are you? Come back! I'm here now!" She listened hard, hoping to hear a scrabble of claws as Truffle reappeared over the fence, but there was only the sound of the wind in the trees. She remembered Mia saying that when Smokey had gone off exploring, she'd been able to tempt him back by rattling his food box. Maybe the same thing would work with Truffle? It was nearly time for her tea so surely the little kitten would be hungry.

She nipped in to grab the box of kitten food, then came back outside shaking it. "Truffle! Truffle!" she called, gazing into all the shadowy corners of the garden. It seemed to be getting darker by the minute. "Where are you?"

The wind rustled through the trees and shrubs, making Molly shiver. Truffle didn't appear. Molly walked further down the garden. "Truffle! Come on, sweetie!"

She caught sight of Truffle's collar on the lawn – it had fallen off again! – and stuffed it into her pocket. So much for Mum buying her a new collar this week –

she must have forgotten. "Truffle! Truffle! Where are you?" she called frantically.

After a while, Molly's mum shouted that it was tea-time, but Molly wanted to keep on looking. "She'll be fine," Molly's mum assured her. "She came back the other night, didn't she? Cats like going off on their own. She'll come in when she's hungry."

Molly held up the collar accusingly. "I found this in the garden – it's come off again!"

Molly's mum turned, looking guilty at Molly's discovery. "I'm sorry, love, I meant to buy a new one, but it slipped my mind," she said. "I'll get her one tomorrow morning. Promise! But come in for tea now. Truffle will be back soon, I'm sure."

"Our cat's always wandering off," Luke's friend Joel put in helpfully. "She disappeared for two days once, but came home again in the end."

This made Molly feel worse, imagining Truffle disappearing for two whole days. How would she cope on her own for so long?

After tea, Molly and her parents went outside with torches to try and tempt Truffle back in again. Molly called her kitten's name until she was almost hoarse. Even Luke came out to help, but

unfortunately he accidentally let Harvey into the garden with him. Harvey started barking excitedly as if this was all a big game, and Molly winced at the sound. If Truffle was anywhere nearby, Harvey's woofing would surely send her running away again! She could feel tears gathering and tried to blink them back. Why hadn't Truffle come home? Was she lost? Or was it that she didn't want to live with Molly any more?

Chapter 6

Molly really didn't want to go to bed that night. How would she ever be able to sleep, knowing that Truffle was somewhere out in the dark, all alone? But her parents insisted that she went up at nine o'clock. "You wait, she'll be back when you wake up tomorrow, I'm certain," said her dad, tucking her in.

It took Molly ages to fall asleep, and when

she finally did, she slipped into a strange, anxious dream. Truffle was lost and miserable, in snow-storms and on busy streets, meowing piteously. Molly was running to her rescue, but she was never quite able to find her. At last Molly woke up, her heart pounding.

It was still early but Molly got out of bed at once, desperate to know if Truffle had come home. She raced downstairs and into the kitchen, hoping to see her kitten in her cosy cat bed, curled up and fast asleep. But the bed was empty, and felt quite cold to the touch. Molly had the horrible feeling that Truffle hadn't been in all night!

Molly burst into tears. She'd only just woken up, but this was already the worst day of her life. She ran straight out into the garden in her pyjamas and bare feet, even though it was a bitterly cold morning. "Truffle!" she wailed. "Where are you? Come home!"

A blackbird fluttered out of the tree at Molly's shout but other than that, the garden was still and empty. Molly stood there with tears running down her face, not knowing what else to do. Had she lost Truffle for ever?

Molly's mum heard her crying and came downstairs to comfort her. "It's not that unusual for a cat to stay out all night,"

she said. "Give it a while longer. I'm sure she'll come back soon."

"But what if she's lost?" Molly sobbed. "Without the name tag on her collar, nobody will be able to get in touch with us to say they've found her. What if we never see her again?"

Molly's mum hugged her. "I feel really bad for forgetting the new collar," she said quietly. "I'm sorry, Molly. But let's try to be positive. She'll be back soon."

Molly wished she could be so certain. After a breakfast she barely tasted, she got dressed and went up and down the street calling Truffle's name. Lily saw her through the window and came out to help, but there was still no sign of Truffle. "I'm worried something awful has happened,"

Molly said miserably. "What if she's got run over?"

"Don't think like that," Lily said, hugging her. "She'd be too scared of the noisy cars to go near the road. She might have got shut in someone's shed or garage, that's all. I bet she'll be back later."

Both girls had to go in for their lunch soon after, but Molly wasn't hungry. "This is all your fault," she told her brothers, glaring at them over the table. "If you hadn't been playing loud music or nearly squashing her with your rollerblades, or scaring her away by shouting, she'd still be here."

Luke snorted. "What are we supposed to do? Tiptoe around so we don't upset your kitten?" he said sarcastically. "We do live here too!"

"Come on, Molly, it's not their fault she's missing," Dad put in. "I know you're upset, but blaming people isn't going to help."

Molly's mum stroked her hair comfortingly. "Once Truffle's a bit older, I'm sure she'll be more confident and less scared of everybody's noise," she said. She put a

little bag in front of Molly. "Here," she said. "One new collar that fits even the smallest of kittens. We'll put it on her as soon as she gets back."

"If she ever does comes back," Molly said, feeling tearful again.

By the time the Kitten Club girls came round that afternoon, Truffle still hadn't reappeared, and Molly felt desperate. "What if someone's catnapped her? Or what if she's hurt somewhere, and can't make her way back?" she fretted.

The other girls were upset too. They couldn't begin to imagine how anxious Molly must be feeling.

"Have you asked the neighbours?" Mia suggested. "When Smokey ran away, we knocked on all the doors in the street. Mrs Jackson said she'd seen him, and then I could tell which way he'd headed."

"Maybe we could print some 'Missing Cat' notices and post them through people's letterboxes," Ella suggested. "Maybe even stick some up on lamp posts."

"Good idea," Molly said. "Let's get some leaflets printed and deliver them to all the houses around here. And I'll ask Mum to knock on their doors with me later on."

Molly turned on the computer and wrote a notice. "LOST! Tabby kitten, 4 months old." She added a photo of Truffle and the Evans's phone number, then printed out the leaflets.

After checking with her mum that it was
OK to go out, the girls split into two groups,
posting the leaflets through all the front
doors on Molly's street. They all called
Truffle's name as they went and kept a
lookout. But there was still no sign of her.
It was as if Truffle had vanished into thin air.

Once they'd delivered their leaflets, the
girls trooped back to Molly's house, all
rather subdued. They did their club roll-call
as usual, and wrote their news into the
scrapbook, but everyone was too worried
about Molly's kitten for the usual laughs and
chatter. Where could Truffle be? She'd been
missing for nearly twenty-four hours.

They tried to distract themselves by
working on their magazine, but nobody was
really in the mood. Then, when it was

almost the end of Kitten Club, there came a
knock on the door. "That's probably my
mum," Ruby said. "She told me she might
be a bit early as she's picking my brother up
from a party first and coming straight here
afterwards."

She went with Molly to the front door –
but it wasn't Ruby's mum standing there. It
was Mrs Flynn, the old lady who lived three
doors away … and she was holding Truffle!

Chapter 7

Molly's mouth hung open for a second in complete surprise, and then she burst into tears, though, this time, they were tears of joy. "Oh, Truffle!" she wept, taking her kitten from Mrs Flynn. "Mrs Flynn, you found her! Thank you so much!"

Molly's mum and dad came to see what all the commotion was, as did the other

Kitten Club girls. "Oh, thank goodness,"
said Molly's mum. "Thank you, Mrs Flynn.
Come in and have a cup of tea. Where did
you find her?"

Everybody went into the kitchen while
Molly's dad put the kettle on. "Well, she's
been coming into my garden for a few weeks
now," Mrs Flynn explained, sitting down.
"She's been my little friend; whenever I'm
gardening, she keeps me company." She
smiled at Truffle, who was rubbing her head
against Molly's arm and purring. "As she
wasn't wearing a collar, I thought she must be
a stray so I started giving her titbits to eat."

Molly's mum looked guilty. "Her old
collar was too big and kept falling off," she
explained, passing Mrs Flynn a cup of tea.
"We've got her a new one now, though," she

said. "Quick, Molly, let's put it on right away."

Mrs Flynn sipped her tea. "Well, this little one – Truffle, did you say her name is? – appeared at the window last night meowing so I let her in, and she snuggled up on the sofa all night. I'm sorry, dear, I didn't realize she was yours otherwise I'd have brought her back sooner." She looked apologetically at Molly. "I didn't even know you had a kitten. I just thought you had a dog."

"I've only had her a few months," Molly said, carefully fastening Truffle's new

purple collar around her neck. It looked very smart. "She's not been going outside for very long – that's why you haven't seen her." She stroked Truffle, who purred even louder, and a thought crossed Molly's mind. "Ahh, I bet that's why she hasn't seemed hungry lately as well," she said. "She's been eating at two houses, not just one!"

Mrs Flynn looked rather awkward. "Oh dear. I must confess, I've enjoyed her company. I do get rather lonely, living on my own. I won't feed her again, though, now that I know she's yours."

"Thank you," Molly said. "I'm just so glad she's all right."

"Me too," Lily said, squeezing Molly's hand.

"Me three," Amy added.

Molly and her friends went upstairs with Truffle. Molly felt exhausted with relief. "Phew! Truffle, please don't do that again," she joked, but then she realized something awful. Chances were, even if Mrs Flynn stopped feeding her, Truffle would still go to her house. Well, why not? It was probably way quieter there than Molly's home, after all.

She lay on her bed, watching as Ella and Mia waggled their fingers for Truffle to pounce on. She would just have to get the rest of her family to help make their house more kitten friendly, Molly vowed. She had to!

Otherwise, Truffle might decide she'd rather move in permanently with Mrs Flynn – or anyone else who'd have her.

Later that day, when her friends had gone home, Molly told her parents and brothers that she was calling an emergency family meeting – right now! Everyone looked at her in surprise. As the youngest member of the family, Molly had never done anything like this before, but Truffle running away had shocked her into action.

"I don't think our house is a very nice place for a kitten to live," Molly began, stroking Truffle, who was sitting on her lap. "We're all so big and noisy, and she's still small and a bit nervous of us. I really don't want her to run away again because she doesn't like it here."

"Well, what do you want us to do about it?" Luke asked, rolling his eyes.

"Alfie could stop blaring out his music for starters," Molly said. "And you could be more considerate of her when you're rollerskating, or if you're in the garden when she is. Like, not kicking a football at her and nearly knocking her out of a tree!"

"It was an accident!" Daniel said huffily. "I told you!"

"Well, I think Molly's right," her dad said unexpectedly. "You boys are old enough to go and play football in the park now, or at the coaching club after school, rather than wrecking our garden or crashing about in the hall. Never mind Truffle, you nearly scared me to death when I thought that football was about to smash through the front door."

"And I agree about the music," Mrs Evans said. "Alfie, I've told you so many times to keep it down. You'll have to start wearing headphones from now on."

"Thanks, Mum and Dad," Molly said. "I'm trying to keep Harvey away from Truffle when she's eating and when she's out in the garden too."

"We'll put Truffle's food up on the kitchen counter," her mum suggested. "That way she can jump up to eat there but Harvey won't be able to get at it."

Molly nodded. "Good idea," she said. "I just want Truffle to be happy, and feel like her family cares about her."

"Sounds reasonable to me," Molly's dad said. "Don't you think, boys?"

They mumbled their agreement, looking sheepish. "Thanks, everyone," Molly said, feeling much better. She stroked Truffle, who purred loudly, as if she felt much better too.

Chapter 8

For the rest of the weekend, everyone tried
their hardest to keep the house calmer and
quieter. Molly moved Truffle's food bowl
on to the counter and she soon got the
hang of jumping up there when she was
hungry. Molly's mum made it a new rule
that everyone had to take their shoes off in
the house, so that their footsteps wouldn't

be so loud, and Alfie wore headphones when he listened to music. On Sunday afternoon, Molly's brothers were sent out to take Harvey on a long walk so that Truffle could have some time in the garden with just Molly for company. They had a great game playing with the bouncy ball with no disturbances.

"This is more like it, right, Truffle?" Molly said, stroking her happily.

Prrrrrr, went Truffle, rubbing her head against Molly's legs as if agreeing.

Later on, while Truffle was snoozing in Molly's bedroom, Molly and her mum took some flowers round to Mrs Flynn's house as a thank you for bringing Truffle back.

"How kind of you!" Mrs Flynn exclaimed in delight. "Come on through."

It was quiet in Mrs Flynn's house with just the slow tick of the clock and the kettle boiling to break the silence. Molly could see why Truffle had liked coming here! She felt a bit sad for the old lady that she didn't have anyone to keep her company. "Have you ever thought about getting a cat yourself, Mrs Flynn?" she asked politely.

Mrs Flynn smiled. "It's funny you should
say that, Molly," she replied. "I was just
thinking the same thing. I've enjoyed having
your little Truffle around. Maybe it would be
a good idea to have a pet of my own."

"The cats' home in town is always
looking for new homes for its strays," Molly's
mum said. "If you do decide to get a cat, I'd
be happy to drive you there to choose one."

"That's not a bad idea," said Mrs Flynn slowly. "I'll think about it. Thank you."

The following Saturday morning, Molly had a special errand to run with her mum. Mrs Flynn had decided that she *would* like a cat, and had asked if Molly and her mum would help her choose one from the cats' home!

Of course Molly had said yes. "Did you hear that?" she said to Truffle, crouching down to stroke her. "You might be getting a new friend moving in up the road!"

Molly's mum laughed. "Well, I don't know about that," she said. "Cats aren't generally very friendly towards each other. They don't like other cats to be on their 'patch', so Mrs Flynn's cat probably won't be all that welcoming towards Truffle." She shrugged. "But that might actually mean Truffle stays closer to home, which wouldn't be a bad thing."

"That would definitely be a good thing," Molly agreed, scratching Truffle behind the ears. "The closer to home the better!"

Molly felt excited for Mrs Flynn as they walked into the cats' home. Mrs Flynn had already had a home visit from someone at the centre, to make sure that her house was suitable for a cat to live in. Now it was the fun part – choosing a cat!

Molly, her mum and Mrs Flynn were shown into a large, light room, which had two tiers of cages along one side. Each cage had a door at the back which led to an outside space. Some of the cats were asleep,

and some were outside. Others gazed out at the visitors curiously. There were cats of all colours – black, white, ginger, tabby and tortoiseshell. Each had a card on their cage with their name and age on.

"This one's called Hector," Molly said, reading the card of the nearest cage. A black and white cat was inside it, jumping up at

the bars. "He's two years old. Hello, Hector!"

"This is Rosie," Molly's mum said, peering at a small tortoiseshell cat with a fluffy tail. "She's very pretty."

Mrs Flynn was smiling in at a small black cat with bright green eyes. "Tabitha," she read on the card. "Just like a witch's cat. Hello, Tabitha."

Tabitha meowed and padded over to see
Mrs Flynn, pressing her head against the
bars as if she wanted to be stroked. "She's
friendly," Molly said, coming to look.

"She's a very nice cat, Tabitha," said the
lady who'd shown them in. "Really sweet-
natured and no bad habits."

Mrs Flynn put a finger through the bars
of the cage and stroked Tabitha's head.
Tabitha purred loudly, squeezing her eyes
shut. "She's lovely," Mrs Flynn said. "Just
the sort of cat I wanted."

And so Tabitha came home with Mrs Flynn that morning, along with a new green collar, some food bowls and cat food, and a grooming brush. Mrs Flynn seemed delighted with her friendly, purring pet, and it gave Molly a warm, happy feeling inside.

"I don't think she'll feel so lonely any more," she told her friends later on at their Kitten Club meeting. This time they were at Ruby's house, and were finishing off their magazine in the living room, while Ziggy, Ruby's crazy kitten, played around their feet. "I don't know who looked happier – Tabitha or Mrs Flynn!"

"Ahh, that's really nice," Ruby said. "I think you should write that up as a news story for the magazine, Molly. I love a happy ending!"

"And what about Truffle – is there a happy ending with her too?" Ella asked. "Has she decided that home is the best place to be after all?"

Molly nodded. "She's definitely spent more time at home lately, since we've kept her and Harvey apart. And now that Alfie's not playing his music so loudly, she knows she's always got a quiet place in my bedroom, where nobody will disturb her." She smiled at her friends. "Me and Truffle, we just shut the door on everyone else and snuggle up together. We've *both* got a happy ending, I reckon!"

Have you read...

Ginger's New Home

Smokey's Great Escape

Ziggy's Big Adventure

Honey's New Friend

The BILLOW MAIDEN

GUPPY BOOKS